SECRET SKIES

K. M. PERKINS

CONTENTS

CONTENTS

CONTENTS

SECRET SKIES

First I would like to say thank you to all those
who will read what I have written. I hope you
enjoy and like to read them. Perhaps you will
even read them more than once. I hope they make
you think, learn, grow, laugh and love. These
works are from years of thinking, meditating and
evaluating. Some created as quick as a blink and
others refined like a fine bottle of luxurious wine.
Please read the words aloud and even in front of a
crowd. These words were written for me and you.
I hope you can see right through them like I see
you too. What is life without a little bit of fun?
Let the words take you on a journey to where ever
you may want to go! Let the words glide from
your mouth and make you feel like you are a

miraculous gift. Let the words reach you where no one can! Feel free to laugh and shout out loud! Share them with your children, your family and friends! Take the book and the memories ever where you go. Thank you cause you are incredible even more than you know. You are magical! For non native speakers these works are a deal! Use these works to improve your English, vocabulary, pronunciation, memory and more! Hope a lot of excitement is in store for you and you speak and converse with ease. Let these words guide you and make you feel wonderful as a snow cone, shaved ice or a roller coaster ride. Thank you one and all hope you have a ball!

I give special thanks to my dear mother. I thank my entire family and my true friends. I give special thanks to J.K.R.

Thanks for the inspiration!

Please
ENJOY!
Read!
Repeat!
Believe!
Sincerely,
K.M. PERKINS

My SKY

I awoke early to view my sky
Gracious blue, the sun glowing into bloom
Fluttering, chirping, liberated birds
Set above soft sailing clouds
Fresh air filling my lungs
Reeling pacific ocean and mountains
A collage, vibrant, animated
Shimmering Beautiful

I awoke early to view my sky
And I was aghast at the sight
Dirty dingy gray and swirling smoke
A barren plain, devoid of pleasure
Inanimate, life none that was visible
Only a skeleton of the past
Fragmented, striped to the bone
Abominable

I awoke early to view my sky
A clean canvas
And with a brush and some paint

I brought it to life
First, the sun and then the fluffy clouds and light
blue sky
Next the great mountains, trees and ground
Two soaring birds
My Sky

Secret Chocolate Sky

Waves of chocolate flowing to astound
Filling the sky with chocolate rays at dawn
Stand taste and feel this unlimited meal deal
Luxuriously lovely addictive seductive
Calling your name
Written in chocolate above the clouds
Ride it, touch it, consume it to know
You got the richness to be smooth
Bars of chocolate gold
Kisses of chocolate cause you are bold
Rain drop truffles trickle on down
Extraordinary elaborate chocolate thunder
Labyrinth sounds
Chocolate hurricane nothing is mundane
No reasons to strain
Reeling in delight
Release your fears and grab hold
Timeless random reminiscing dark white
caramels
Caress cascade
Chocolate trees and chocolate seas
Sensational sensual sexy passionate fusion
Chocolate magnanimous missiles soar through

the skies

Landing lightly chocolate syrup surprise
Triple chocolate fudge infinity
Honey coconut Kona coffee
Chocolate macadamia nuts
Bedazzle the night
Radiant red raspberries chocolate cherries insight
Chocolate skyscrapers rise into the clouds
Exponentially amazed and revolutionary
Chocolate Bill of Rights
You have the right to remain in the Chocolate sky
We hold these truths to be self evident
Life Liberty and the pursuit of fabulous fantastic
chocolate fantasy sky

Secret Skies

Speaking without words
Walking without walking
Hearing the unheard
Seeing the unseen
Music in the mind
Linked internally
Visions of the Secret sky
Viscous violent venom
Striking stealth-fully
Fluid ferocious movements powerful as the sun
In the river
In the mountains
Where the stones stand above the clouds
Out like a candle
On like a fight
Still as night
Rapid as right
Wild woken warriors bound by no limits
Within the waves of the secret sky
Spherical symmetrical illusions of Yin and Yang
Overlapping animal spiritual realm
Ancient American Indians lands

Alive in the slanted seven secret skies

Totem to totem
Tiki to Tiki
Titan to Titan
Tellus to Tellus
Terrace to terrace
Thunderbird to Thunderbird
Realm to realm
Faster to faster
Master to master
Reverse to converse
Verse to verse
Collapse it to surpass it
A mass it to contrast it
Sigma Theta Beta Secret Sky

Desire to Run

Woke before the sun to go for a run
My breath like smoke
My feet like fire
Just pure desire
Frost was soon lost
Each stride took me higher
Ground to sky was the divider
Rays beyond pierced the horizon
Always hope!

Frozen Delight

On frigid nights
Along arboreal corridor
Bubbling brilliant bright
Transcending worries or despair
Caressing crescendo
Distant dancing dreaming
Embrace juvenile carefree
With open arms
With open hearts
With open mind
Each step in
Enhance enchanting

Insomnia

Streets stand serene
Suspended amplified animation
Translucent trails
Just trying to fall asleep
Go with the beat
Footsteps on the bed
Echo in my head
Walk in the hallow crickets to follow
Fade in fade out
Next stop
Deep sleep
Repeat

Solace

Dark clouds park
Round sound found
Down all around
Rain drops dabble
Fall to ball
Call a drawl
Down surround
Smooth sooth solitude

Rainy Day

Spurt spatter spray
Cars speed on down the way
Chirp Chirp Chirp
Birds chatter
Children giggle gaits
Pitt-er patter plop
Drops start stop

February Nights

Breath of frost
Hands of stone
Feet of ice
Frigid night delight
Pavement a stride
Stars sparkle wink
Full moon blooms
Plays me a tune
Symphony epiphany
Breath of glitter
Mind like ice
Pure February nights paradise
Devious delusions
Frozen tears
Quick freeze dry
Delirious frost bite
Arctic Vortex solidify
Lethal as knife
Lethal as a dagger
Stop you dead in your tracks

Methodical

Some say it's a crime
To make a rhyme
All the time
Like a chime
So sublime
Like a mime
An infinite prime
Repeat!

Wonder Night

Astride on ice
On frigid night
Street a snooze
People loving booze
A cloud sky high
A dragon in disguise
Cross great divide
Watch wonder whirl
Emblazon twirl
Destination set
Smart stutter set
Onward North Star
Leaping frog
Not far behind

One Stride

Memories set aside
Come out to take a ride
Echo in sound
Break it all down
Buzz to a bee
Sonic to bat
Set the direction
Wandering waves
Land on vast shores
Pave the way
Open the way, just gone astray
Infinite affinity
Sail on away...
Happy sunshine day!

Fruity

Papaya and mango
Like a tango
Smooth and sweet
What a treat!
Without the heat!
Intrinsically unique!

A Drink

I find no pleasure in the glass of man
Devoid of pragmatic priorities
In moments of praise and folly
At the rim of mediocrity
A toast to one and all
I find no pleasure in the glass of man
Blasted in tone and deeds
Rally rebelling boasting to the break
Light in head as in heart
I find no pleasure in the glass of man
The foolish face of praise
You span to break glass and the standard
And never, never fade...

Sequence Sound

Alone I sat to think of nothing
Then I thought is nothing always nothing
Or is nothing sometimes something
And nothing can be nothing
Why nothing is nothing more than something
Sea to sea, something of nothing
Ocean to ocean, nothing of something
They do converge
Knowing you know nothing
Means you must know something
And something of nothing
Exceeding the limits of nothing
Quite extraordinary

Midnight Hustle

Awake in my sleep
Distantly Dreaming
Deep drastically distantly
Reeling emotions
electric as lightening
Poised like a Viper
Ready to strike
Repeat...
Fluid flames illuminate ignite

Snappy Smooth

Silent sinister silky sleek
Light desires to flame
Astounded astronomically
Streaming stars tonight
Tantalizing tingling
Tenaciously tonight
Aimlessly Koed tonight
Fragrance fanatic
Frantically fragrance
Wet insatiable appetite

Motivation

When the lights are out
When the fridge is bare and this is your third day
without a meal
When your pockets are empty but the rent is due
Horrifying not hypothetical
When everyone is out to get you cause they can't
muster the strength or intellect to do it
When you are told it can not be done
When the jinx is long as hell
When you are the long shot 1000 to 1
Your passion compels
Motivation to break the spell!
Motivation to unleash
Mind boggling
Thunderstruck
Dumbfounded
How?
You managed to pass the test
How?
You managed to transform a no win situation

To whimsical, wonderful win!

How?
You managed to make your dream reality
Motivation to make it happen
For all the damage you inflicted on me
Mentally and physically a Punic Victory!
Motivation to the max
Passionate perspective methodical leverage
Happen it can
Unmistakably unanimously to do what they say
can't be done
Rise to the challenge
Miraculous motivation

Magical Friend

You are round sound found
Inspirational as light
Bring me insight
Take me on a magical flight
Soaring spectacle delight
Courage to fight
Right as bright
East to west
North to south
Sensational stretch
Like stars shinning at night
You guide me higher
Make me desire
Feel like fire
Magical moment
Miracle magic
My secret magical friend

Affinity

Something to hold
Something to untold
Uncanny cunning
Remote running
Stalking stunning
Avarice appetite...

Sky Vision

Arrows flow into the sky
Pathway to free the waves
Mysterious mist in a haze
As beautiful as the emeralds in her eyes
The sea rises and soars into the sky
Strength to embrace
Stand, plan, build a magnificent vision
Infinite sky vision
Evolutionary or
Revolutionary?

Knowledge

Rise to know
Rise to gain
Rise to create
Rise to think
Rise to learn and never be the same
Gain to know passion to grow
Know to earn unlimited potential
Experience innovation light insight
Pandemonium peering sensing magical miracle
direction
Steering storing building knowledge
Knowledge to add knowledge to love
Love to evolve
Love to knowledge
Knowledge to live knowledge to survive
Maintaining sustaining Ascending
Inspirational beautiful knowledge
Enlightenment
Revolutionary lovely powerful knowledge

Magical Love

Magical beautiful lyrical love
Lyrical miracle magical love
Making miracle love
Sensational passionate love
Miracle lyrical magical love
Infinite magical miracle love
Inspirational lyrical love
Miraculous love
Lyrical miracle infinite love
Living love
loving living
Lyrical miracle magical love
In the sun
Under the full moon
Living lyrically
Lyrically living
Miracle lyrical moonlight love
Intoxicating addictive in a spell
Eating half as much
Thinking and loving twice as much
Loving through the day and night

The road to health and wealth

Mischievous melody of love
Miracle lyrical magical love

Speed to Win

Driven to excel
Driven to propel through hell
Driven to push the extreme limits
Beyond pain
Beyond the sane
Driven to cross the great divide
Putting the petal to the metal
Putting it all on the line
Break the sound barrier
Break the race barrier
Maximum propensity
Leveling opponents
Leaving them in the dust
Against the impossible
Ready to amaze
Reset the guidelines
Redefine, redesign creativity innovation
Demonstrate
Make the inconceivable goals
Speed to win

Champion

Today I stand to dream
Today I imagine beyond
Nothing shall bind my spirit
Nothing shall bind my mind
Nothing shall bind my body
What Where When Why
Desire to live!
Courage to fight
Desire to innovate
Desire to innovate
Desire to soar beyond the horizon
Desire to pierce the clouds into space
Feel the determination
Feel the passion of love
Love for my lost ones
Let the force guide me
Let the force release me
Achieve the impossible
Live in the light
Live through the dark
Achieve the unachievable

The Aviator

The sky calls to me
The sky waits for me
The clouds welcome me
The stratosphere reaches for me
The sky yearns for me to take off into it's vastness
Soar like the eagle
Soar like the hawk
Focused concentrated on the horizon
Fly at Mach 3
Flying freely fluidly beyond
With hope, with excitement, with love
With infinite passion for the dream
For the desire to fly swiftly
Desire to achievement
Desire for independence
Live in the skies and on the horizon
Sun rise and sets with me
Timeless as the seas
Timeless as the Blackbird...
Legendary as the Tuskegee Airmen
Legendary as my Uncle Les
Determined to fly

Proving anything is possible in the sky
In your imagination
As in mine..

Magical Sands

In the sand
In the dessert
The pebbles, the stones the particles breath into
life
The particles that form breath life into the sands
The life flows through the sky
The sky forms the shapes that build the blocks for
the next game
The air fills with it
The air is complete
Magical particles
Magical light emits the waves
That flow in the night
Waves that dominate ones sight
Sands of magical time

Invisible Man

Look here
Can you see
In the brilliance of daylight
Or in the shadows lurking in the night
Pressed tightly into places
Submerged in vivid void
Transparent, an amorphous sheet
Gesticulating responding to the game
Gleaming distorted bursting into flames
Responding programmed familiar for fame
White-lights when it's white's turn
Black-lights when it's black's turn
They verify the mode
An illegal move boy!
Damnation to your soul
Corralled by rippling bars
Coated to the bone
Beneath blood is an ebullient tide
Advocate of translucence deceptive to touch
No feeling to reminisce
Feelings are currents returning to the shore
Imagine the predicament not being seen

Excruciating punishment for knowing too much
Liberation
Emerge from the unfathomable
Shake and shed thy virulent sheath
Cleanse thyself of the stench
Regenerate
Resurrect
And leave
Contents:
One hide
BBQ Artificially flavored

Giant Star

Just a small twinkle in the endless galaxy
Unknown to the world
A star so bright
So brilliant
And so beautiful
It could light the whole world
But is today the day
Or must I wait
To feel the warmth, love, and passion
Of the giant star
For if I must I shall wait
I will not fade
I will shine for the fight
Stand and make it right
Embrace the infinite beauty of the Giant Star

Sunflower

A day born to drift
Shifting clouds
Shifting stars
Shirting seas
Shirting mental realities
Stand clear
The sun is here
Releasing cascading vibrant rays
Bursting through
Boozy, woozy lovely lullaby light
Reaching far and wide
A bloom tune
Melody majestic
Equity enlightenment
Luminous linear perceptive
Searching soulful sailing
The Sunflower

Mr. Crow

At sunrise so wise so wild
What do you say Mr. Crow?
What can you see Mr. Crow?
Up at dawn
Dancing, prancing, making some noise
Looking for seeds
Looking for grubs
Looking for hidden jewels
Gleaming glitter
Glittering diamonds untold
Where are they Mr. Crow?
Where will you find them?
Where will you walk?
Where will you fly Mr. Crow?
Oh!
It's a mystery miracle Mr. Crow
What do you know Mr. Crow?
Your mischievous and lyrical as the wind
Give me a sign Mr. Crow!
Do you really know?
Is it all just a fluke?
It's a mystery

Say hi Mr. Crow
So sublime, plenty of fly time!
What do you know Mr. Crow?
How can you know Mr. Crow?
There is no denying
There is no prying
Who is it Mr. Crow?
Set everything right
Let us know Mr. Crow
So courageous, benevolent and wise
What do you really know Mr. Crow?

Super Blood Wolf Moon

Mystical mutant moon
Full in the night
Covered in blood
A ghoulish delight
Plastered to the wall
Playing with fire
Like gangbusters you hit the scene
Surreal impressionistic modernism
All jacked up
Frivolous flat line folly
Ammunition all-nighter
Catch it while you can
Focus, shoot and take it
Rare as they come
Astonished bemused
Super Blood werewolf moon

Spirit of the Ocean

A raindrop falls on the mountain
A raindrop falls on the lake and rivers
A raindrop falls on the pavement
A raindrop falls on your head
All heading destination Ocean
The ocean holds the incredible life force
The treasure of fish
The treasure of luminescent plankton shinning in
the moonlight
Beautiful magical coral
The miracle of birth
The miracle of waves swallowing the silhouetted
shores
The miracle of dolphins communicating at ultra
high pitch sounds
Communicating with deep diving whales
Vicious ferocious sharks lurking beneath surface
Feeding on schools of fish
Manta rays glide on the mysterious particle
bubbles
Above the multicolored coral carpets
Sea turtles emerge from the sands

Struggling against the elements and predators at
hand
The sea turtle is wise, strong and inspirational
Traveling vast distances on the ocean tides
Ecstatic in the estuaries teaming with life
Infinite invisible legendary light life force
Building into a undeniable powerful perfect wave
Like a hurricane
like a Tsunami breaking unleashing punishing
blows
Unstoppable stronger than the will of any man
The Ocean life force
We all breath it
We are born with it
We all flow with it
Yearn for it
Oceans live with us
The life it supports
Supports us all
Let us live like this
Let us reunite like this
Let us cherish it more
Life to support the spirit
Live to fight for it
Live to soar, flow, and dream

Realize the Spectacular Spirit of Ocean Waves
Spirit love life ocean

Toils Spoils of the Thief

Oh! What do you say to a thief?
Stealth-fully stealing your fruits of labor
In your house when the lights are out
Or in your car, phone, computer, and bank
Oh! What do you say to a thief?
Oh! What do you do to a thief?
Do you catch and quick release a thief?
Some say yes
Some say no
Some say nevermore
Oh! What do you do to a thief?
Stop right there don't go anywhere cause you're a
complete thief!
Quite contrary
Some say lay them down
To rot in the dirt
Cut them in half and feed them to the hogs
Oh! What do you say to a thief?
That makes false illustrious promises
Growing fat on the toils and lobbies of others
hard labor
Filling their pockets while others flip flap torment

to die
Sticky fingers to get their unlimited cut
Oh! What do you say to a thief?
Oh! What do you do to a thief?
Stealth-fully stealing your arduous fruits of labor
Make them work twice as long to replace what is missing
Make them pay 1000 times more!
Or seize all their assets
Oh! What do you do to thief?
Catch them red handed
Today's the day the thief must pay for their actions!
Oh! What do you say to a thief?
Oh! What do you do to a thief?
Perplexing puzzle predicament

Ephemeral

One day upon a casual passing
I took note of long beautiful passage
Strolling down
There rose such a splendid portrait
A shimmering red bridge that was arcing
Converging with multicolored leaves surround
My heart astray wanted to meet it
Full of joy and exuberance I stride to
My windfall vanished before I knew what to do
And until this day I still do seek
A sleek red bridge that's quite unique

Fragile Wings

Far below I did ascend
Step to step
Dream by dream
Building that I knew not of
Faded spaces rich beneath my feet
Existing nowhere on the globe
Rising from fragile gilding
To become my greatest stronghold
Stars ride my wind to the sky
Climbing ceaseless slanted slopes and vertical
walls
Brick by brick
Blood by blood
Resisting the force of stone
Bearing the gift
Level to level
Broken weariness no longer a foe
Soaring lowered, smiling to myself
The solemn stair no further to go...

In the Light

Exalted above it lies
Reeling into an infinite light blue emerald sky
A raging war
An arsenal of dark and sight
Good and bad
Life or death
Strong and noble
And yet golden at that
In the light of truth it lies
Sometimes fall astray
Hoping, wishing to fathom
Viable on not facts clarity
Differing on latitude
That decisions past
Reign as truth and not just hyperbole

Haiku

Underneath the mist
Liberal leaves change color
Exalted high up

Behind setting sun
Majestic sails ride hard wind
Glide beyond this sea

Upon the great wave
Riding frees the Hawaiian
Exempt from the city

In the clear blue sky
Cherry blossoms fall gently
On the still water

Above the great clouds
Snowflakes cool to the touch fall
Upon the old mountain

Under a full moon
Graceful fish travel currents
Through coral branches

Beneath gold sunlight
Fragrant petals open wide
In a spring meadow

Before the sunrises
Water droplets fall silent
Around the mountain

Hawaii Calling

Hawaii is a calling
Warm trade winds blowing coconut trees
Soothing Sunshine leis
Welcoming hula girls swaying to and fro
Lushes chocolate honey dipped Kona coffee macs
Smiling inviting faces greeting you with Aloha
Oh! Hawaii is a calling
From everywhere
In the day and night
Longing for me to return to Waimea
Surfing pacific waves
Longing for me to ride horses in the valley
On the Kualoa Ranch
Sailing above the Na Pali Coast
Straight to the wondrous waterfall Waimea
Canyon
In every way
The Spirit of Mana, Ha, Ohana, Aloha Way
Fireworks illuminate the night
Hot delicious Hawaiian food on a golden platter
Precious potent Koa House pancakes pack a
powerful taste bud wallop

Chinese, Korean, Indian, Thai, any food you
name it!
Milky Way Stars burst across the skies of the
Kilauea Military Camp
Snow capped Mauna Kea rising in the distance
Mokulua Islets sunset
Plate lunch picnic before Diamond Head in the
day in Kapiolani Park
Oh! Hawaii is calling!
Walking on the sands of Waimanolo
Wading in the warm blue waters
Washing away every worry
What more can I say
Oh! Hawaii is a calling
And I am on my way!

Trees of The Future

Resilience, strength, vitality and propensity of the
tree is undeniable
Let us look to this strength
Growth slow, steady, long and deep
Roots diffuse, disperse and dynamic
Supporting the tremendous weight
Supporting effective efficient ecosystems
Hundreds, thousands and millions
Absorbing CO_2
Releasing life giving oxygen
Providing shade and shelter
Providing fuels for fires
Providing useful paper
Intense inconceivable
Linked to our evolution
Our primordial ancestors
Let us stand to protect the wonderful magical
magnetic power
Planting the seeds to nurture the majestic trees of
the future

The Gift

What is the ultimate gift?
The gift to elate
Make you gravitate
The tangible intangible unknown
What is the ultimate gift?
Sunshine satellite
Moon beams out of sight
Waves that entice
Winds that satisfy
What is the ultimate gift?
The lights of dawn
Courage to know you can achieve your dreams
Dedicated, determined and driven
Eyes exceed animosity
Let nothing hold you back
Focus, visualize, refocus, and revitalize
Confident discipline extraordinaire
What is the ultimate gift?
Today, tomorrow, and everyday
You are the gift!
Maximize your full potential

You are what you perceive yourself to be...
A multi-Talented Authentic Gift
Love to win
Win to Love
Make it fun
Make it count
Make it what you want to be
For I am the Gift
You can be too
Live, Think, Plan, Build, Recreate, Fight and
Protect
I am and you can be the Greatest you can be

The Sky Tree Dream

Run the course
Iliad Odyssey, Treasure Island, Shogun
Tale of Heikei
Sea Wolf, Captains Courageous, stay the journey
Through all obstacles epic
Simultaneous tempests
Twisted spiraling vertigo steel
Cruising for a bruising
Cool bananas
Cool to the core
Calm cool collected
Ecstatic Erratic Die hard Engineering feat
Eclipsing Predecessors reaching for the stars
Reaching for the universe
The Galaxy to hold
Central, Milad, Oriental Pearl, Shanghai, CN,
Canton Towers
Blown away
Upside down obsolete
Run that by me one more time!
Run the course

Run the gambit
Stay the journey
Periodical placement prioritized
2,080 Meters
Number one under the sun
Stretching screeching Supersonic safely
elevator ride
You must be high!
360 sky deck day vision digitized
Tokyo Tower, Ryogoku, Edo Tokyo
Hakubutsukan
Mountain Fuji Surprise
Remarkable go haywire
Go full throttle to my and the sky tree dream
Put the pedal to the metal
Start your engines
Restart your mind
Brains not brawn secure the future
Infinite dividends float in the sky
Returns on mental investments
Hundreds to Thousands to millions to billions can
and will be realized
Visions of athletes going for the Gold, Silver and
Bronze

2020 of Tokyo Olympics on this horizon will
unfold
Like elaborate origami
Music melody meticulously laid
Singing skeptic suspense Comic book animations
Dragon Ball
Interwoven Kimonos, Yukata, Hapi, Matsuri
Magnificent
Robots bionic subatomic video game sporadic
actions
Intrinsic value
In the money
Reflecting amusement Acura, Lexus, Infinity,
Altima, Camry, Corolla
Laughter sustain strain VR surreal
What's the deal?
Celestial sushi, ramen, gyudon, sukiyaki,
Teppanyaki, Sushi
And more!
What's the dream?
Capital, equity, assets, revenue
Fortified at the sky deck
445-450 floor
Plans made
Checkmate Mr. Park

Expression experience extend
Here there and everywhere
Now what?
My sky tree dream is reality
Now take yours to the top
Envision precision correlate
Fundamental sentiment psychological
Too mundane value added
Dynamo shinkansen super express magic bullet
train ride
I got my ticket
Get your ticket too
Let's radical race to the pinnacle
Departure to infinity
My sky Tree Dream
Skykp23

My Black Hawk Song

Two shadows in the distance
Enticing as the sun
For here or to go?
Business or pleasure?
Riding the warmth of spring winds
Silhouette serenade
Embers substantial supreme
Straight talk
Riding on each others trails
Landing in Sakura trees
Breathing in fragrant Sakura petals bloom leaves
Enigmatic eloquence
Two shadows in the distance
Enticing as the sun
Supersede side by side
Hail to the Noble!
Hail to the courageous Black Hawk!
Bound by no one under the skies
Proud as freedom
Proud as love
Proud Predator of the skies

Independent as the stars
A true G of nature
Shattered only by shots in the air
Torn apart by a hunters snare
Mate blown apart filled of buck shots
Hail to the Courageous Black Hawk
Bound by no one in the continuum
Black Hawk, Black Hawk
Can you hear?
Black Hawk rides and calls on the winds
Seasons follow him on his wings
The sun rises ans sets with him praising his name
Black Hawk, Black Hawk Immortal Son

Feeling the Love Song

There's a full moon in the night
Time to risk a flight tonight
Waking to walk in the midnight streets tonight
Feel the Magical Love tonight
Feeling the beat
Feeling the love
Feeling the hidden waves tonight
Feeling the magical tonight
Gliding in the sexy sky
Reaching for miracles of love tonight
Feeling the magic
Feeling the love
Feeling the moon
Taking me higher
Taking me farther than I have ever been tonight
Feeling the beat
Feeling the love
Feeling the magical spirits tonight
Feeling your soul
Feeling the beat of love tonight

Hot as fire Potent as desire
Feeling your love tonight
She is mischievous
Longing for me tonight
Waking to walk with her tonight
Electric eyes
Listening to her love tonight
Feeling the harmony
Feeling the heat
Feeling the beats
Feeling the magical love tonight
Time to risk it all
Time to jump for love tonight...

RAD (SONG)

Rad to the moon
Rad to the sun
Rad to the night
Rad to the life
Rad to make it out of sight
Rad to the way
Rad to the day
Rad to what you say
Rad to monkey around
Rad to the speed of sound
Rad to make it snappy
Rad to make it VIP
That's who we be
Rad to fireworks
Rad to the bright
Rad to the lights
Rad to the spectacle
Rad to Rad
Rad to the right
Rad to the max
Rad like a Nitro blast

Rad like a bounce
Rad to pounce
Rad to Rad leave you in the dust
Let's make it a trust
Rad to the stash
Rad to the Rad
Rad to the max
Rad to the works
Rad to the limit
Rad to the positive
Rad to the pessimist optimist surrealist
Rad to the brilliance
Rad to the spectrum
Rad to the mega
Rad to galactic
Rad to the real deal
Rad to rad rad to no anchors
Rad to the max millions. billions, and trillions!

Doko Ni Ikitai no? (SONG)

Iku saki wa naisho
Iku saki wa shorai no yumei
Iku saki wa katamichi kana?
Iku saki wa ofuku kana?
Iku saki wa nariyuki
Migi Hidari Masugu na michi ja nai kara
Chika michi no naisho
Doko ni ikitai no?
Itsu ni ikitai no?
Dare to ishoni ikitai no?
Do yate ikitai no?
Subete wa naisho
Naisho wa subete
Zetai ni oshienai naisho
Naisho wa naisho dakara
Doko ni ikitai no?
Naisho nariyuki no naisho
Yumei no naka no naisho
Eiin no naisho
Naisho wa eiin
Omoshiroi subarashi kagayaku naisho

Naisho wa naisho dakara
Doko ni ikitai no?
Giri giri naisho
Mo ichido
Iku saki wa yuwanai naisho
Get my drift!
Caveat Emptor Co gito ergos sum

Adonde Va?

Adonde va?
Es secreto
Secretemente secreto
Solamente secreto para manana
Cuando va?
Adonde va?
Quien va contigo?
Es secreto no puedo a ensenar nada
No se
Ahora no se nada
Siempre es secreto
Secreto es secreto aqui, alli, por todas partes
a la esquierda, a la derecho, directamente
Es secreto
Puedes a creer
Creer a poder
El sueno es secreto
El lugar es secreto
Soy repentista
Soy criador
El viaje es secreto

Solamente secreto
Porque?
Porque secreto es siempre secreto
Queire a comprendir mas?
Es secreto

Joetsu Shinkansen

Ueno Station
Track 19
ASAHI 323
Down two ways
Forward and aft
Humming, strumming electric rumbling
A quick last dash for a drink
Long sounding alarm
And all aboard!
Pressure mounts to a hiss
As doors to a close
And we're on the way
Welcome aboard the Joetsu Shinkansen
Super Express train bound to the North
Not much bread
So I'm in non-reserved, non smoking
None the same
Feeling fine
Through the mountains
Through the tunnels
Silent snow

Hovers in the skies
As we pass on by...

Sands

Sun be still
The waves are in
Cast away the known
Begin to grow
Shifting grains
Gradually pass the heat
Intensify
Join the beat
Colors
Fresh vibrant mind blower
Smoke and mirrors
Off the wall
Have a ball
Wheel an deal
Double, triple whammy
On the same wavelength
You could have knocked me over with a feather
Run down some lines
Or I'll lose my grip like quicksand
On the fast track

Zigzag
Zoom in
Ala Moana
At the beach
On the waves

Recap

World are you ready?
What's up?
Do you recall?
Do you know what you have read?
Hope you got this far
If you did you are a Super stellar star
And really enjoyed the whole enchillada
Hope your mind has been blown
It knocked your socks off
And not your covers
Do you remember the time?
Hope you do and didn't cut and run
Did it read well?
Did it feed your mind?
Recall Recall
Yeah! Total recall hope you had some
It's better than being between a rock and a hard
place!
For if you did don't you fret
It's time to tee off

There's nothing but clear sailing from here on out!

Clear skies
Hope you realize your dreams
Right here
Right now
Right here in the Secret skies
Adios, Gracias, Hasta manana!
Sayonara
Arigato! Ja mata!
Xiexie! Taibang la!
Let's meet again sometime!
Miten menee?
Kiitos! Olet mahtava!
Danke!
Hope you read and reread them again and again!

Hey! Surprise... Check out the bonus features!!

Bonus Feature #1
Taco Bell and Burger King Hell

Hey what duya wanna get?
I'm up for anything!
How about Taco Bell?
No way!
What duya mean?
I got sick as hell at Taco Bell
That is why I never eat it!
Ordered two beef burritos and a side taco to go
Tasted great as I chowed it down
Too bad I didn't know
Was in for more than I could chew
In 30 minutes I had a bazooka blast
that registered on the Richter scale
Oh! I got sick as hell at Taco Bell that's why I
never eat it!
My mega blast plastered the walls
Nearly split my rear
Runs were no fun and lasted day and night
I nearly lost my sight
Oh! I got sick as hell at Taco Bell that's why
I never eat it!

Are ya up for Burger King?
No categorically NO!
I got sick as Hell at Burger King!
That's why I never eat it!
Ordered a juicy flame broiled Whopper to go
I was licking my chops anticipating the flavor!
Chowed it down nice and slowly on the
walk home to soak in the taste
Within 20 minutes depth charges detonated in
my stomach
Ran so fast to get to the toilet I could have
beaten Bolt
In the bathroom stall I tossed more than my
cookies
Felt like meals for three days came up and out my
mouth and nose
Oh! I got sick as hell at Burger King that's why
I never eat it!
Barfed until closing time
I still see it in my nightmares
Hacking, Barfing and blowing out that whopper
Until this day I never ever never ever eat
at Burger King or Taco Bell!

Bonus Feature #2
Woman Biathlon Skier
copyright © 2019 K.M. PERKINS

Infinite determination at -25 below
Brilliant untamed sexy inner beauty
Unyielding spirit against the frigid elements
Intense interval training
Skiing through shadowy solitude night
Skiing to compete
Driven to push the limits of metaphysical
stamina, endurance, fatigue
Aiming lethally at distant targets
Playing skillfully the cards she's been dealt
Setting your sites
Steel nerves
Nerves of steel hallmark of a champ
Beating the clock
Striving forward
Going for the Gold
Make no mistake
All the glories yours
In the streets before dawn
Wild dreams
Wild sexy Ice

Wild dreams
Bi-athlete Reality
Burning like jet fuel
Leap breathing linger
Lungs hunger oxygen
Muscles masquerade madly
Mind mummified Amaze
Stupefied glace
Arms pumping like pistons
Fighting forward furiously
Wild dreams
Wild Sexy as Ice
Wild untamed reality...
Mina Rakastan Sinua!!

Bonus Feature #3
Tennis Champion
copyright © 2019 K.M. PERKINS

Rise to hit the road
Running through the streets to release
Gain greater stamina
Greater speed to feed the need
Hitting the weights
Hitting the shots
Visualizing raising in the ranks
Astounding arsenal
Miraculous serves blazing the court!
Aces and winners cross court down the line
Ferocious forehands
Brutalizing backhands
Victorious volleys
Every moment living for each point
Amazing drop shots, over heads and lobs
Focused on the ball
Focused on the goals
Focused to break the mental
and physical barriers
Disposing each opponent

With cunning determination
Challenging to win
Challenging to exceed expectations
Beyond your lateral limits
Challenging to never give up!
Fighting every point
With unfathomable unimaginable will to win
All rise to be a Tennis Champion
Roger Federer
My friend indeed

Bonus Feature #4
Above the Rim (SONG)
copyright © 2019 Kevin M. Perkins

Above the rim!
Imminent sky
Imminent take off
Imminent shake off
Banking it in! Arcing it in!
Slamming it in! Jamming it in!
Above the rim!
Making it HOT!
Above the rim
Skillfully stepping
Skillfully dribbling
Skillfully passing
Stop stutter step synthetic
Pumping it up!
Above the rim!
Stepping it up!
Above the rim!
Leveling it up!

Street beat driven elite
Street beat driven to compete
Above the rim!
MJ Making his moves
Making his marks
Making his sky waves
Magical Improvisation
Streaking across the nation
Above the rim!
You can make it show!
Above the rim!
You can make it pop!
Make it drop!
Make it crop!
Above the rim!
Light it up!
Snap it up!
Bounce, pounce and eat it up!
Above the rim!
Rhythm range rectify
Mobile Mad Mystify
Electric Fission Energize
Zigzag zoom
Above the rim!

Dancing direct digitized
Dishing down delivery
Cashing dashing magnified
Above the Rim!
Came to win!
Above the rim!
MJ Unlimited
MJ sky way
MJ HEY Day!
Above the Rim!
What you say?
Above the rim!
Infinite heat
Infinite beat
Infinite combat to compete
Above the rim!
Came to win
Came to dominate
Came to navigate
Above the rim!

Bonus Feature #5
Mystical Journey

Where do you want to go?
Where the sky carries me
Where the wind wakes with me
Where the waters magnify with me
Where the sounds echo with me
Where do you want to go?
Where I can walk above the clouds
Where the sun rises for me
Where her fragrance radiated for me
Where the calls of the wild awaken me
Where the ocean and the skies touch the horizon
Where do you want to go?
Where no one will know
Where everyone desires to go!
Where I can make the impossible possible
No when, where, what or why
Where I can fly higher farther longer
Where do you want to go?
Where you do not know
Where no one knows

Nor anyone will every know
In the space between space
On the points between points
Along the lines between lines
Where do you want to go?
Go where I go to know
Know where I go to unknown
To the mountains within mountains
To the rain within rain
To the winds within winds
On the journey within a journey
To the sand within sands
Tell me to tell me
Let's go!

Bonus Feature #6
Coffee Skies

Welcome one and all to the Coffee skies!
Wake before dawn
Rising with the Coffee Sun
Aromatic amazing American
Aphrodisiac Arabica
Brilliant Carnival Samba Brazilian
Delightful dazzling medium dark roast
Sensational Sexual Canephora Coffee
Rich satisfying tantalizing tropical Colombian
Collaboration Coffee Robusta
Extravagant to the max Kopi Luwak
Original official Ospina
Enticing Everlasting Esmeralda Gesha
La Fiesta por la Vida Fazenda Santa Ines
El injerto Peaberry
Jiving High as the sky on Jamaican Blue
Mountain
Los Planes is especially for you

Hawaiian Kona Coffee Volcanic manic
Lighting you up
Coffee Skies
Raining fine luscious coffee grounds
Lovely luxuriously living large
Coffee rivers flowing
Oceans of coffee brewing
Waves of liquid coffee rushing to the shores
Delirious density caffeine coral
Coconut coffee trees
Even humming coffee bees
Homemade Handcrafted Heavenly coffee
Espresso Coffee skies
Let's keep it up
Let's keep it LIVE!

Bonus Feature #7
EMAAR on Top of the World

Technical Titan
Groundbreaking striking
Streaking above the skyline
Spectacular spellbinding
Dubai Creek to Dubai Square
Mega magnificent magical vision
Mind blowing optical performance precision
Riding inspirational innovate decision
Mirror image of a falcon in flight
Astounding astronomical sight
So grand it must be right
Reflecting the sky by day or night
EMAAR on Top of the World
Infinite Confidence to Free the Mind
So incredible it must be Divine
Liquid Light Living Large love LED show
Dream believe dare determination DO
Doing the Destination
Big time Big talk Big Exhilaration
Lifting you and your spirit higher than the sky

EMAAR on Top of the World
Showtime Extraordinaire 163 floors
Burj Khalifa 2,717 feet
Just you and me!
Open to the Imagination
WE CAN!

SECRET

SKIES

FOREVER!
SECRET
SKIES
FOREVER!

www.ingramcontent.com/pod-product-compliance
Lightning Source LLC
Chambersburg PA
CBHW030355180626
46812CB00007B/2891